Once Upon A Time series:

Snow White

Concept and design:	Edward Glover
Typesetting:	Dave Organ
Production:	Johnson Lane
Audio recording:	Hat's Off
E-book production:	Innovations by Design Ltd

ISBN: 978-1-898250-20-3

Printed book: manufactured in China

10 9 8 7 6 5 4 3 2 1

E-book: produced in India and manufactured in China

Camelot Editions is a division of Transedition Limited
Oxford, England

Snow White

Original story by the Brothers Grimm

Retold by Sally Byford

Illustrated by Angela and Eric Kincaid

CAMELOT EDITIONS

Once upon a time...

on a winter's day, a queen was sewing by an open window.
She pricked her finger on a needle and a drop of blood fell
onto the snow below.

"I wish for a daughter with skin as white as snow, lips as red
as blood and hair as black as ebony," she whispered.

When her wish came true, the king and queen were overjoyed.
They called their baby Snow White. But the queen died suddenly
and the unhappy king married again. His new queen was the most
beautiful lady in the land. She was also vain and cruel.

The queen had a magic mirror and every day she asked it,

"Mirror, mirror, on the wall,

Who is the fairest of them all?"

The mirror always replied,

"You, my queen, are the fairest in the land."

But as the years passed by, Snow White grew prettier and one day the mirror gave a different answer.

"My queen, you're beautiful, it's true,

But Snow White is more beautiful than you."

In a rage, the queen summoned the woodcutter. "Take Snow White deep into the forest and kill her!" she screamed. The kind woodcutter was horrified, but he couldn't disobey the queen. So next day, he led Snow White deep into the forest. As the sun began to set, they stopped in a clearing.

"You are in great danger," whispered the woodcutter. "The queen has ordered me to kill you." Snow White's eyes widened with fear. "Run away and hide," said the woodcutter. "I won't hurt you." Then he returned to the palace and presented the queen with a pig's heart to prove that Snow White was dead.

Snow White felt lost and alone in the gloomy forest until a friendly robin chirped at her from a nearby tree. It flew a little way and chirped again. Snow White thought it was saying, "Come with me, come with me." She followed the robin along a winding path until she came to a cottage in a clearing.

No one answered when Snow White knocked, but the door wasn't locked and she tiptoed inside.

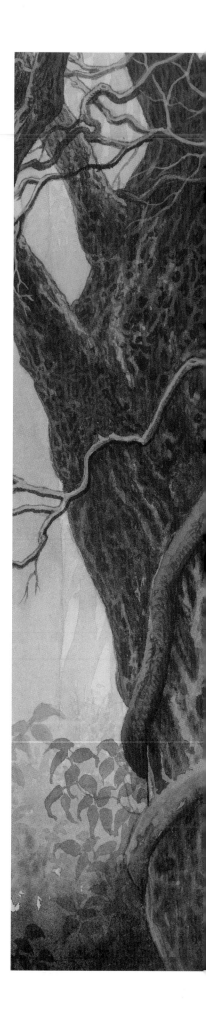

Snow White was weary after her long walk. She crept up the creaking staircase and found seven little beds. She lay down to rest on the biggest bed and was soon asleep.

Before long, seven little men returned to the cottage from their work in the mines. They were surprised to find a beautiful girl asleep upstairs. Snow White was even more surprised when she awoke to see seven little faces all staring at her. "Don't be scared," said the kindest little man. "We won't hurt you." Snow White told the little men her story and they begged her to stay.

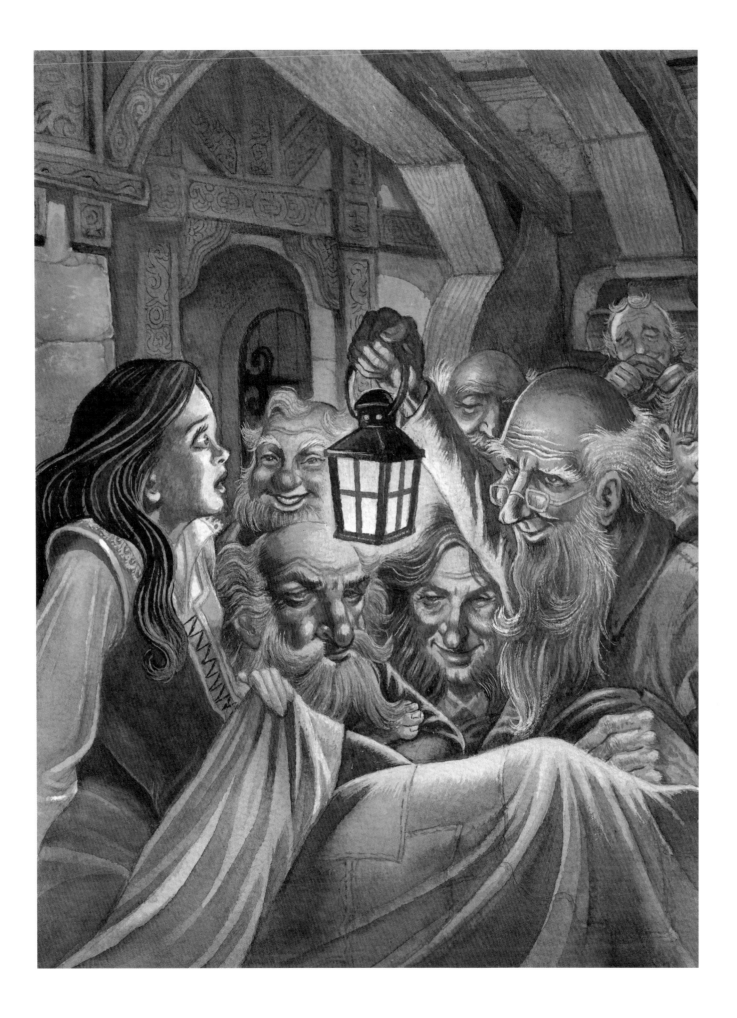

Back at the palace, the queen asked her magic mirror,

> "Mirror, mirror, on the wall,
>
> Who is the fairest of them all?"

The mirror replied,

> "My queen, you're beautiful, it's true,
>
> But Snow White, living in the glen
>
> With the seven little men,
>
> Is far more beautiful than you."

The queen grew scarlet with rage. She threw the woodcutter into a cold, dark dungeon and plotted to kill Snow White herself.

The very next day, the queen crept out of
the palace disguised as a peddler woman.
She hurried into the forest and found the
cottage where Snow White was hiding.
As soon as the seven little men had left
for work, she knocked on the door, crying,
"Ribbons and laces for sale!"

When Snow White saw the woman's basket
of colorful ribbons, she invited her in and
bought a bright red lace for her bodice.

"Let me lace you up," said the peddler woman.

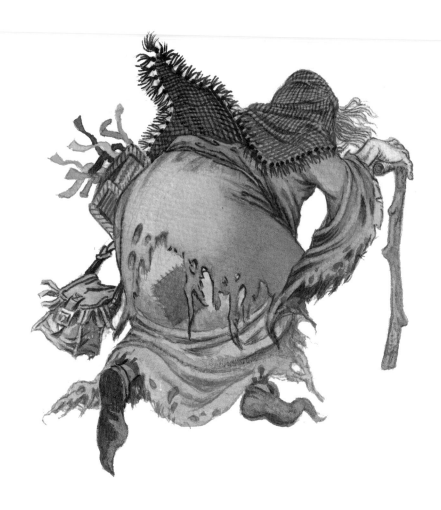

The queen pulled the lace so tight that Snow White collapsed on the floor. "That's the end of you, my pretty!" she cried. Then she wrapped herself in her black shawl and scuttled back to the palace.

When the little men came home, they found Snow White lying on the floor as though she was dead. But the wisest little man quickly unlaced her bodice and Snow White soon recovered.

"This is the queen's doing!" said the little men. "You must take care, Snow White. Don't open the door to anyone."

When the queen discovered that Snow White was still alive, she prepared a poisoned comb and hurried back to the cottage in a different disguise. Snow White was already alone, so the peddler woman knocked on the door, calling, "Pretty combs for sale!"

Snow White opened the door a crack. "It's only a peddler woman," she thought. "What harm can she do?" And she opened the door wider to look at the combs.

"This one would look lovely in your dark hair," said the peddler woman.

She picked out the poisoned comb and stabbed it into Snow White's hair. In an instant, Snow White fell to the ground. "Farewell, pretty princess," screeched the queen.

When the seven little men came home, they found Snow White lying by the open door. The wisest little man quickly pulled the poisoned comb from her hair and Snow White soon recovered again.

"The queen is clever, so you must beware," said the little men. Snow White promised not to open the door to anyone ever again.

The queen soon found out she had failed again. She took an apple and filled half of it with powerful poison. Disguised as an old beggar woman, she hurried to the forest with a basket of apples and knocked on the cottage door. Snow White didn't answer, so she rapped on the window, calling, "Rosy apples for sale!"

Snow White peeped out of the window. She couldn't believe that this poor old woman would harm her, but she had promised not to open the door to anyone. She opened the window, just a crack.

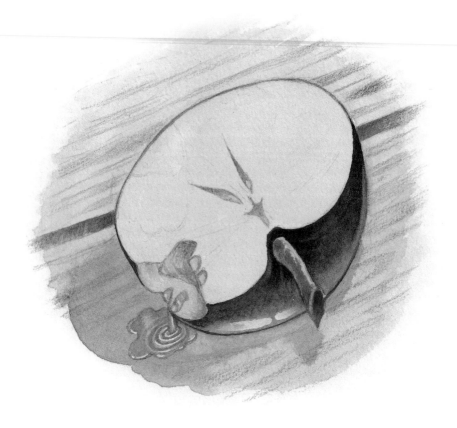

"Please try a nice rosy apple," croaked the old woman, holding out the poisoned one in her wrinkled hand. When Snow White shook her head, the old woman cackled with laughter. "What are you afraid of?" she said. "Look, I'll eat half and I'll leave you the rest." She cut the apple and handed the poisoned piece to Snow White.

When Snow White saw the old woman bite into her half, she took a bite too. With a cry, she fell to the floor.

"No one can save you this time!" screeched the queen.

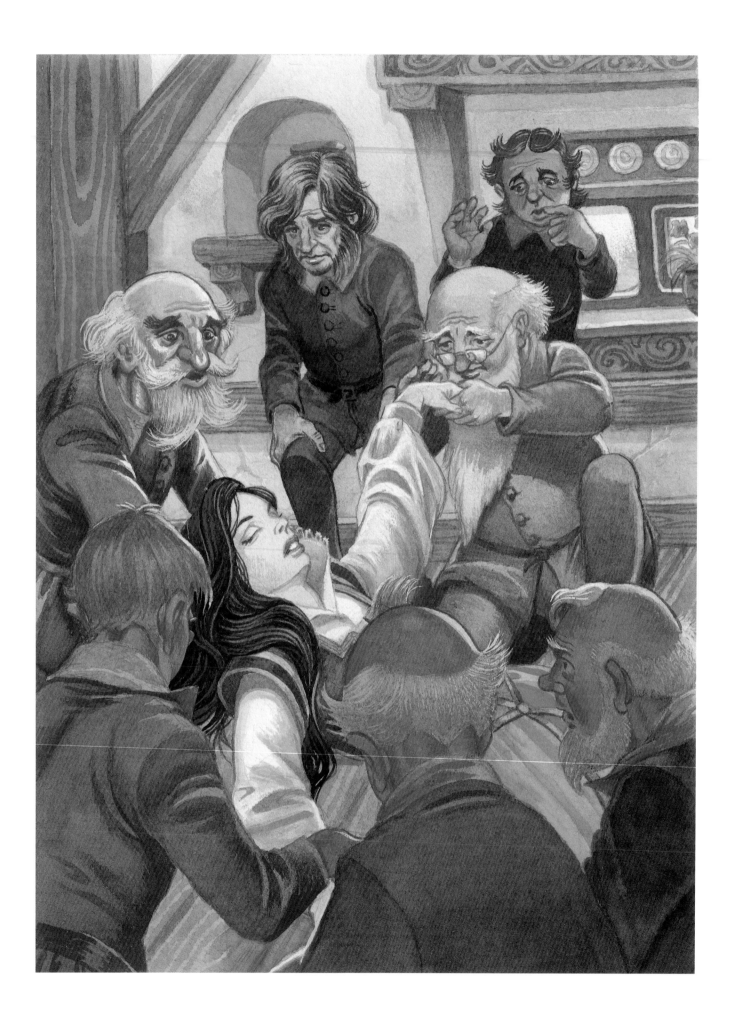

When the little men came home, they tried everything they could to bring Snow White back to life. But not even the wisest little man could help her.

"She's so beautiful," said the youngest little man, "we should put her in a glass coffin so that everyone can see her." They all agreed. So they laid the coffin close by their cottage and took it in turns to watch over Snow White.

Only the wicked queen was happy. Every day, her mirror told her:

"You, my queen, are the fairest in the land."

People came from far and wide to see the beautiful princess in her glass coffin. One day, a handsome prince from a faraway kingdom came riding by. He saw Snow White lying there as though she was only sleeping, and he asked the little men who she was. After that, he came as often as he could to sit by the coffin.

After many months, the prince asked the little men if he could take the coffin to his palace so he could see Snow White every day. The little men were sad to lose Snow White, but they knew how dearly the prince loved her. When they agreed, the prince was overjoyed and told the little men they were always welcome at the palace.

The little men lifted the coffin and carried
it through the forest towards the prince's
palace. Suddenly the oldest little man
stumbled, the coffin slipped from his hands
and the piece of poisoned apple fell from
Snow White's mouth. She slowly opened
her eyes and lifted her head.

The prince was overjoyed and he asked Snow
White to be his wife.

On the day of Snow White's wedding, the evil queen stood

proudly before her magic mirror. But this time the mirror told her:

"My queen, you're beautiful, it's true,

But Snow White, in a kingdom far away,

Who married her handsome prince today,

Is a thousand times more beautiful than you."

In a fit of jealousy, the queen smashed her fist through the magic

mirror and died with her heart full of hatred. Snow White and the

prince lived happily ever after and so did the seven little men.